MOUSE'S
FIRST DAY OF
SCHOOL

Lauren Thompson

Illustrated by

Buket Erdogan

SCHOLASTIC INC.

New York Toronto London Auckland Sydney
Mexico City New Delhi Hong Kong Buenos Aires

To Owen and Graham, best-of-all buddies—L. T.

To Kevin and Alyssa, for all the fun and inspiration—B. E.

ISBN 0-439-68111-1

Text copyright © 2003 by Lauren Thompson. Illustrations copyright © 2003 by Buket Erdogan. All rights reserved. Published by Scholastic Inc., 557 Broadway, New York, NY 10012, by arrangement with Simon & Schuster Books for Young Readers, Simon & Schuster Children's Publishing Division. SCHOLASTIC and associated logos are trademarks and/or registered trademarks of Scholastic Inc.

12 11 10 9 8 7 6 5 4 3 2 1   4 5 6 7 8 9/0

Printed in the U.S.A.   40

First Scholastic printing, September 2004

Book design by Paula Winicur

One bright morning,
Mouse found a hiding place...

that took him to a
brand new space.

Down on the floor,
Mouse found . . .
one,
   two,
      three,
         four
            blocks!

Vrim,
vrum,
vroom

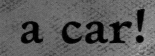

a car!

Up on the shelf,
Mouse found . . .

A, B, C
books!

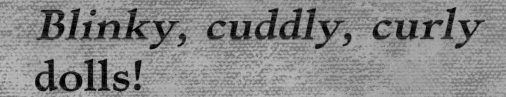

Blinky, cuddly, curly dolls!

Viny, climby, twiny plants!

Over on the table,
Mouse found...

red,

yellow,

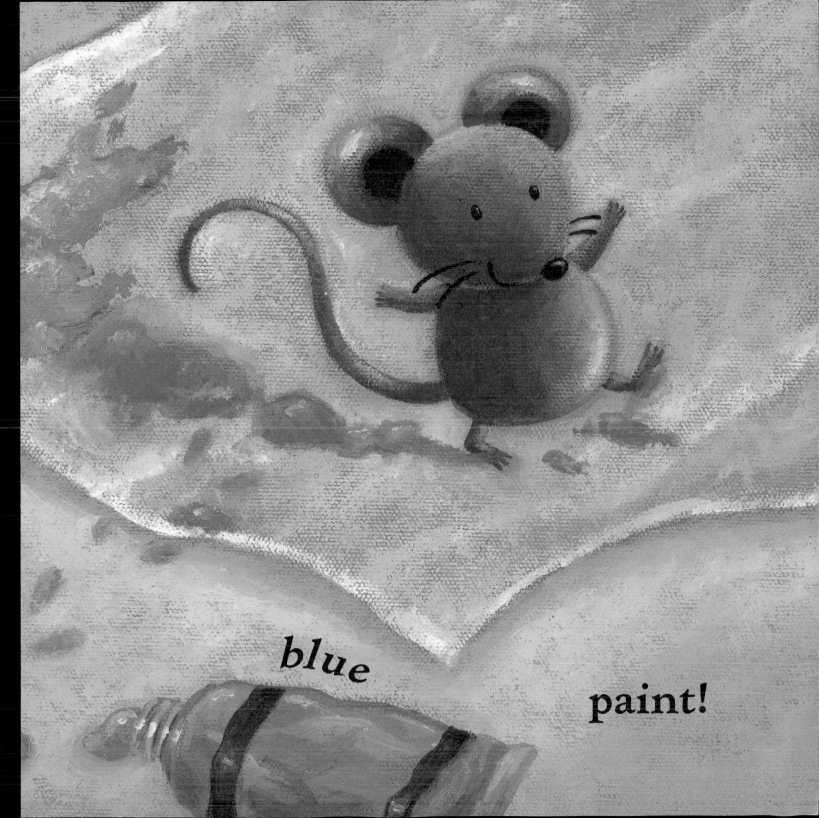

blue paint!

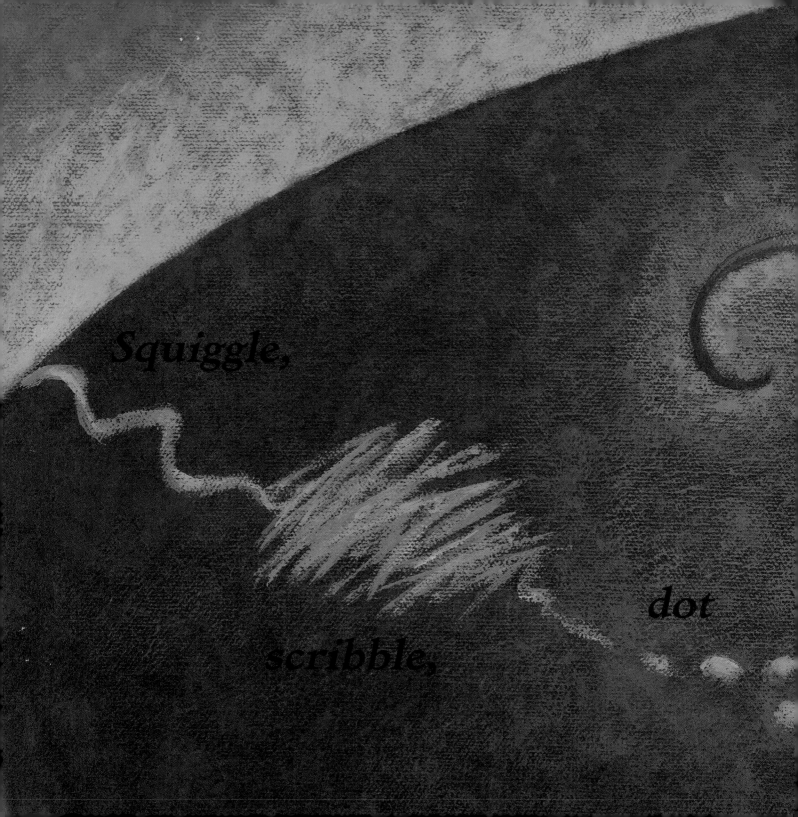

Squiggle,

scribble,

dot

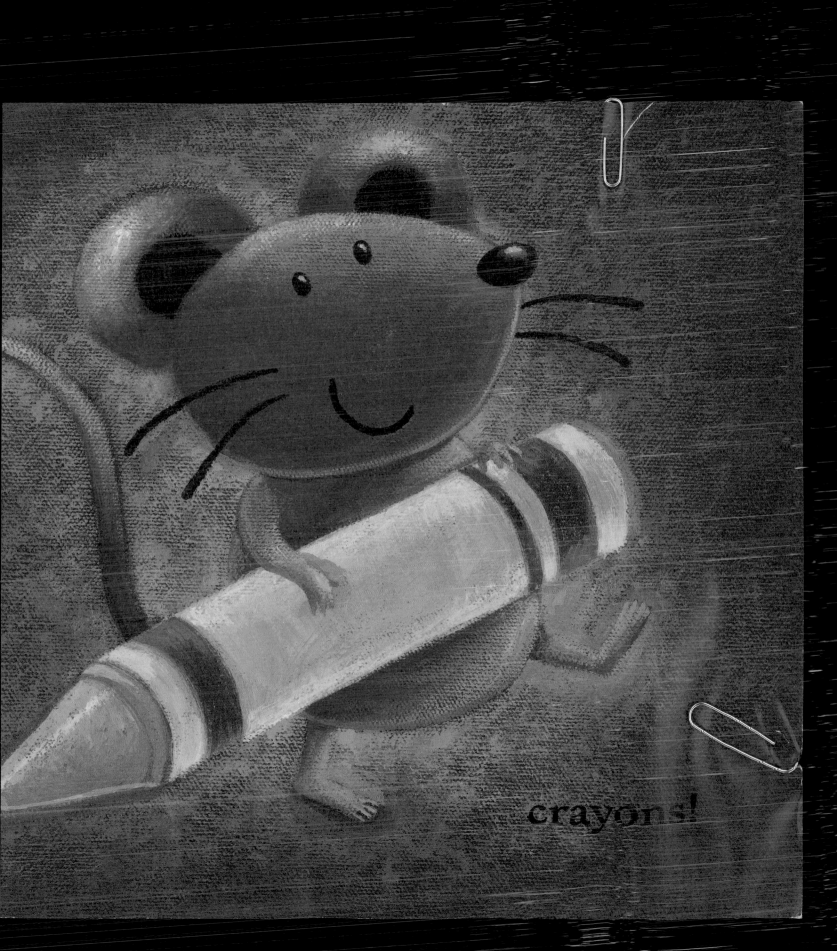

crayons!

snacks!

There in the corner,
Mouse found...

circle,

triangle,

square

Feathery,
floppy,
boppy
hats!

Clang,
bang,
stir

pots!

Then all around,

Mouse found ...

Wiggly, giggly,
best of all
friends!